PUFFIN BOOKS

The Diary of Dennis the MENACE

Beanotown Battle

For my merry band of outlaws:

the 2014 cast of *Lost Boy: The Musical*...

Lauren Cocoracchio, Grace Gardner, Hannah Grace,

Jodie Jacobs, Richard James–King, Natalie Lipin,

Luka Markus, Isaac McCullough, Max Panks,

David Scotland, Joseph Taylor,

Andrew C. Wadsworth, Joanna Woodward

PUFFIN BOOKS

Published by the Penguin Group
Penguin Books Ltd, 80 Strand, London WC2R 0RL, England
Penguin Group (USA) Inc., 375 Hudson Street, New York, New York 10014, USA
Penguin Group (Canada), 90 Eglinton Avenue East, Suite 700,
Toronto, Ontario, Canada M4P 2Y3 (a division of Pearson Penguin Canada Inc.)
Penguin Ireland, 25 St Stephen's Green, Dublin 2, Ireland (a division of Penguin Books Ltd)
Penguin Group (Australia), 707 Collins Street, Melbourne, Victoria 3008, Australia
(a division of Pearson Australia Group Pty Ltd)
Penguin Books India Pvt Ltd, 11 Community Centre,
Panchsheel Park, New Delhi – 110 017, India
Penguin Group (NZ), 67 Apollo Drive, Rosedale, Auckland 0632, New Zealand
(a division of Pearson New Zealand Ltd)
Penguin Books (South Africa) (Pty) Ltd, Block D, Rosebank Office Park,
181 Jan Smuts Avenue, Parktown North, Gauteng 2193, South Africa

Penguin Books Ltd, Registered Offices: 80 Strand, London WC2R 0RL, England

puffinbooks.com

First published 2014
006

Written by Steven Butler
Illustrated by Steve May
Copyright © DC Thomson & Co. Ltd, 2014
The Beano ® ©, Dennis the Menace ® ©and associated characters
TM and © DC Thomson & Co. Ltd, 2014
All rights reserved

Set in Soupbone
Printed in Great Britain by Clays Ltd, St Ives plc

British Library Cataloguing in Publication Data
A CIP catalogue record for this book is available from the British Library

ISBN: 978–0–141–35084–4

www.greenpenguin.co.uk

MIX
Paper from
responsible sources
FSC™ C018179
www.fsc.org

Penguin Books is committed to a sustainable
future for our business, our readers and our
planet. This book is made from paper certified
by the Forest Stewardship Council.

The Diary of Dennis the MENACE

Beanotown Battle

Written by
Steven Butler

Illustrated by Steve May

PUFFIN

FLOWERS!!

STUPID, sniffy, flopsy, wafty, PINKY, STINKY, skippy, drippy, happy, flappy FLOWERS!!!

I HATE FLOWERS!!

After all the exciting things last term at school . . . all the ghosties and fireworks and snowstorms and snowball fights and mouthfuls and MOUTHFULS OF CHRISTMAS CAKE, the only thing we have to look forward to in the spring is FLOWERS!

It's AWFUL!!

Don't get me wrong . . . spring brings loads of **BRILLIANT** menacing things like PUDDLES and MUD and FROGSPAWN.

HA! There's loads of fun to be had with FROGSPAWN . . . Last year, I swapped Dad's porridge with a big bowl of the gloopy stuff when he wasn't looking. He went green for a week when he realized what he was eating . . . Then I blamed it on my little sister, Bea . . . Happy times!

BUT

SPLAT!

it's all spoiled by stupid flowers!!!

Look what Mum left on the kitchen table . . .

CALLING ALL
GREEN-FINGERED
GARDENERS

With spring rushing up
to greet us in its warm,
flowery arms, it's time
to get out into the garden
and plant, plant, PLANT!

EXCITING NEWS: Beanotown is taking part
in a competition to be named this year's

BLOOMING BRILLIANT BOROUGH!

The Mayor wants blossoms on every corner,
flowers in every window and spilling out of
every garden. Get outside, people, and grow . . .

With your help, just think how beautiful
Beanotown will be!

UGH!

THIS IS THE WORST NEWS EVER . . .
EVER!

Oh, wait . . . you probably don't know why it's the **WORST NEWS EVER!**

Well, my MENACES-in-training, since you're reading my brilliant Menacing Diary, I'd say you're about ready to learn the **TERRIBLE** truth about flowers . . .

Flowers attract the worstest, most awfulest, boringest creatures ever to skip across the face of the earth . . . **AND I'M NOT TALKING ABOUT WIMBLY-PIMBLY BEES AND BUTTERFLIES . . .**

NO! SOMETHING MUCH,

MUCH,

MUCH

WORSE!!!!

Are you ready?

Brace yourself . . .

ARRGH!

FLOWERS ATTRACT
SOFTIES!!!

If Mum and all the rest of the CRAZY adults get their way and turn Beanotown into a **BLOOMING BRILLIANT BOROUGH**, Softies will arrive in their millions. They'll flounce here from all over the world! Skipping and tripping and clapping . . .

Me and my dog Gnasher have a hard enough time already, putting up with my BUM-FACED arch-enemy Walter . . .

What am I going to do if the town is overrun by them?!?! What if there's so many, I can't keep up with my menacing?

WHAT IF I START TO TURN INTO A . . .

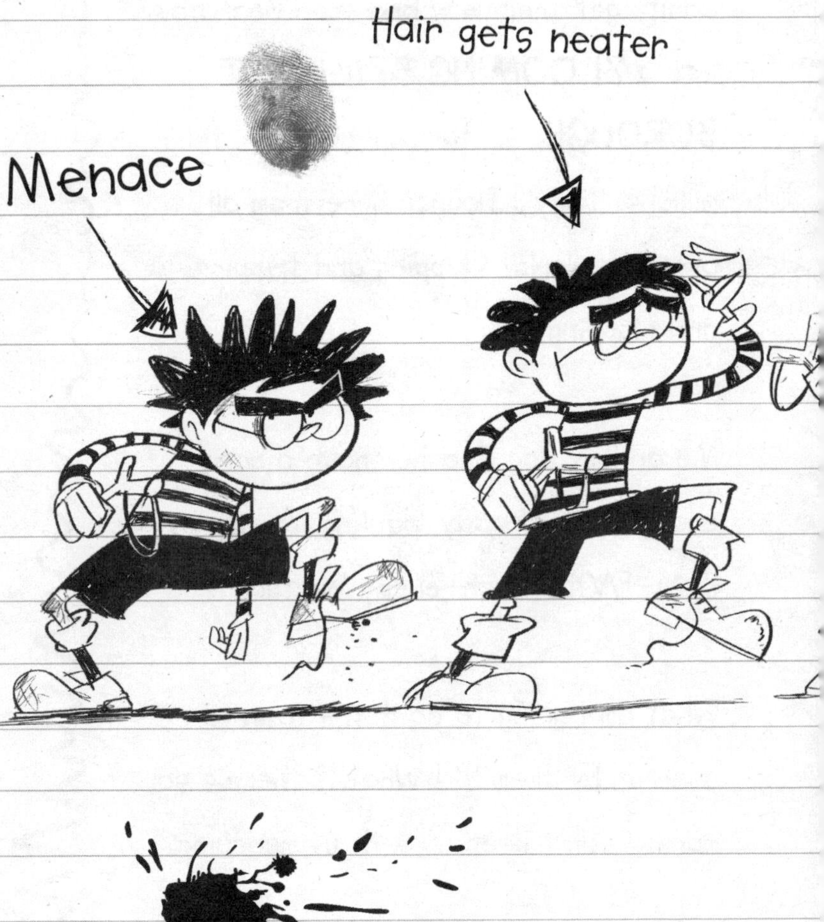
Menace
Hair gets neater

It'll be like something from a **ZOMBIE**
movie . . . only with less blood, groaning and
flesh-eating, and more skipping, giggling and
flower-sniffing.

IT'S TOO MUCH TO BEAR!!

Me and my gang are going to have to come
up with something really, REALLY, REALLY
menacing to stop all those grown-uppy, sappy
BUM-FACES from invading our town.

Me!

Curly

Gnasher

Pie Face

MY MENACE SQUAD

Hmmmm . . . Don't panic. Just leave
it to me. We still have a bit of time before
the weather clears up and all those evil little
flower-sprouts start growing.

It's going to be tough . . .

ANYWAY . . .

Before we can start worrying about the hordes
of Softies that could be heading our way, there
are other terrible things to think about.

Tomorrow is the first day of the spring
term . . .

Yep! Here we go again, back to Bash Street
School. **It's so unfair** . . .

It was at the beginning of last term that my crotchety old troll of a teacher, Mrs Creecher, punished me for not doing my summer homework and made me write this diary for a whole school year.

At first it was torture. I was certain I'd die from diary-dreary boredom, but it turned out **BRILLIANT!** I had the **GENIUS** idea to make my diary into a **MENACING MANUAL** for all you Menace Squad Trainees out there . . . Creecher is going to **BUST HER BONCE** when she sees it . . .

Bored!

~ **UGH!** Of course there'll be the usual

FIRST DAY OF TERM SPELLING TEST

tomorrow. Dad made me come up to my room to

study the dictionary . . .

Bored!

STUDY THE DICTIONARY?!?!

ON THE LAST DAY OF THE
SCHOOL HOLIDAYS?!?!
I SHOULD BE OUT MENACING,
NOT SITTING INDOORS WITH MY
NOSE STUCK IN A BOOK!!

Boring!

Bored

When you're as CLEVER as me, you don't need

to study . . . and anyway . . .

WHAT'S A DICTIONARY?

Boring!

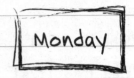

Monday

7 a.m.: Ugh! Well, it looks like my Mega-Bleep-Digi-Clock still works. I haven't had to use it for the whole of the Christmas holidays . . .

7.15 a.m.: I suppose it's not so bad after all! It might be **BUM O'CLOCK** in the morning, but Mum's bought a new box of Poppin' Jammy Sour-Candy Toaster Tarts as a first day of school reward because she thinks I'm writing nice things in my diary. <u>HA</u>!! Grown-ups are so stupid!

Toaster Tarts are the best snack to eat for breakfast **EVER!!**

With a brain—food breakfast like this, there's no way I won't ace my first day of school. Old Creecher will be amazed . . .

1 p.m.: Hmmmmmm . . . I think there was something wrong with those Poppin Jammy Sour-Candy Toaster Tarts . . . Mum must have bought stale ones or something. There's no other explanation for it! It's that or Creecher just marked my test wrong. She **is** getting very old after all . . .

Dennis

Mrs Creecher's Class
Spelling Test

1. BUM-FACE X *Because*

2. Lafter X *Laughter*

3.  X *Dangerous*

4. Clapt X *Clapped*

5. NEVER!! X *Caught*

6. ?

7. BORING! X *Dennis, this was supposed to say 'between'.*

8.  *Dennis, see me!*

17

1.15 p.m.: **_UGH!_** Well, I went and saw the old **GRUMP** and she thinks I wasn't concentrating in my spelling test. How am I supposed to concentrate when we're all being bored to death? REALLY?! I just don't get it . . . I've got far too much to be getting on with. I haven't even come up with my first **BIG** menace of the year yet . . . BUT . . . I think I've got an idea.

You remember that newspaper clipping that Mum left on the table? **YES! OF COURSE YOU DO!!** Well, look what was on the back of it . . .

BIG TOE!

THE SCARIEST MOVIE OF THE YEAR!
CAN YOU WATCH IT WITHOUT WETTING YOUR PANTS?

NEW!

PET PANTS!
AS SEEN ON TV!

A BRAND-NEW MONSTER MOVIE?!?!

WOW, it would be GREAT if monsters were real, though . . . I could train one and Gnasher and me could keep it as a pet . . . BRILLIANT!!

NOT SO BRILLIANT! It looks like Creecher isn't finished with me. Now she's making me spend the rest of lunch writing '**I MUST CONCENTRATE IN MY SPELLING TEST**' over and over again until I fill ten whole pieces of paper . . . Yes, **TEN!!!**

I've done one whole page and it's taken me ages. I'll be dead before I finish NINE more!

HA! If Creecher thinks I'm missing out on jelly and ice cream in the school canteen, she must be more crackers than I thought . . .

Hmmmm . . . Think, Dennis . . .

AHA! No one will mind if I just pop into the school secretary's office while she's gobbling her lunch and use the photocopier . . . That way Creecher will get her pages of lines and I'll get my JELLY AND ICE CREAM . . . Everybody wins!

Menacing Lesson no. (469:)
        Always cut corners!

21

I
AM
A

23

BASH STREET

F.A.O. Dennis the Menace's Parents

It is with great disappointment that I am writing to inform you of a huge disturbance that took place at Bash Street School today.

After he performed extremely poorly in his spelling test, I gave Dennis the punishment of filling ten pages with the line 'I MUST CONCENTRATE IN MY SPELLING TEST' during the lunch break.

Not wanting to do this, Dennis filled one page and then sneaked into the secretary's office and tried to photocopy it ten times.

Unfortunately, Dennis typed in the wrong numbers and ended up photocopying the lines 10,000 times.

The poor secretary got the fright of her life when she opened the door and was buried under an avalanche of paper with Dennis riding on top of it, looking VERY proud of himself. It took us the whole afternoon to dig the poor thing out.

I'm sure you will agree that this behaviour is completely inappropriate and he should be punished accordingly.

I suggest that Dennis should be banned from all ice cream, jelly and other desserts at lunchtime for the whole term.

Sincerely,

Mrs Creecher

Mrs Creecher

NOoooo!!!!!

Midnight: I can't sleep! I keep having dreams about bowls of jelly and ice cream running away from me . . . No matter how fast I run they just get faster and faster and I can't keep up . . . **COME BACK, JELLY!!**
ICE CREAM!!

This IS A
NIGHTMARE!

Where are monsters like **BIG TOE** when you need them? I bet a monster would be a great friend. I bet monsters love the taste of miserable old teachers . . .

{Tuesday}

Dear Diary, I . . .

| Thursday |

I . . . can't . . . cope . . . Three days

without jelly and ice cream . . . **CAN'T GO**

ON . . . will . . . die . . . soon . . . if . . .

I . . . don't . . . taste . . . its . . . yummy . . .

goodness . . .

27

WON'T ... MAKE ... IT ...

I ... CAN ... FEEL ...
MY ... LIFE ...
SLIPPING ... AWAYYYYY ...

DEAD!!

(ARTIST'S IMPRESSION)

Dear Trainee Menaces,

If you're reading this, it's because I **died from lack of sugary treats**. I think it's safe to say that I was **murdered by Mrs Creecher**. After all, who wouldn't die after being banned from all school canteen desserts? Please throw her in **PRISON** for a **squillion years** . . . Oh, and Walter too . . . and Headmaster . . .

Please have my body buried in a giant tub of **butter-banana-chocco-scotch** ice cream and will someone take care of my dog Gnasher for me?

Goodbye forever,

Dennis

Monday

All right, so I may have gone a little bit over the top with the whole dying thing . . . **WHAT?** I was in a state of panic!!

It turned out OK anyway. Every night this week, I've just waited until Mum and Dad have gone to bed and then sneaked down to the freezer in the kitchen to eat my day's share of ice cream. It's like being a secret agent!

So what if I can't eat dessert at school? Mum buys the super-duper good stuff anyway . . .

DOUBLE FATTIES' DOUBLE-FAT ICE CREAM!!

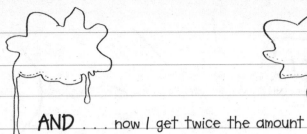

AND . . . now I get twice the amount before bed. It's not ideal, but it's just enough to keep my body alive. **Phew!**

Just don't tell my mum . . .

BUT WHAT AM I DOING?

WE'VE WASTED SOOO MUCH TIME! If you're going to be proper trained **MENACES** by the time you've finished reading this diary, we'd better crack on to the good stuff.

First things first . . . Something

MEGA

happened in the playground today.

There I was, minding my own business behind the bins, when I heard Walter and his posho, bum-faced Softies, Bertie and Dudley, talking.

THE SOFTIES ARE GOING CAMPING ON
MOUNT BEANO WITH THE BEANOTOWN
BUTTERFLIES!!!

That gave me a BRILLIANT idea . . .

Today at lunch I ran into the school canteen
and put my plan into action.

A TROOP OF S.A.S.
COMMANDOS HAS GONE
MISSING ON MOUNT BEANO!
ALL THAT'S BEEN FOUND ARE
THEIR CHEWED-UP TENTS . . .
THE POLICE THINK IT'S THE
MONSTER BIG TOE!

HA! It's so funny . . . Walter and his cronies instantly turned as white as ghosts. I could see them out of the corner of my eye. They're such **WIMPY-WET-PANTS** . . .

Anyway . . . here's the plan.

TOP SECRET!

OPERATION
– MOUNTAIN MONSTER –

Next weekend, Mum and Dad are taking Gran
for a trip to the beach at Beanotown-on-Sea.
They think I'm going to stay at Pie Face's for
the night, but really . . . **REALLY** . . . me
and Gnasher are going to follow Walter and
his Softies up Mount Beano and we're going to
**SCARE THEM SO MUCH THEY'LL POOP
THEIR POLKA-DOTTED PANTS!!!**

This is the best menace I think I've EVER come
up with . . .

It's going to be BRILLIANT!!!

Mount Beano is huge and there are loads of amazing hiding places in the forest. I'll be able to get really close to the Softies without them seeing me . . . and then . . .

KA-BLAM!!

DENNIS AND GNASHER STRIKE!!

All I have is one week to spread more rumours of a monster on the mountain and Walter's gang will be as easy to scare as a turkey at Christmas dinner!

BRILLIANT!

Wednesday

10.30 a.m.: Ugh! Operation Mountain Monster is going to have to wait a little while. Today is going to be a long day . . .

It's our 'lesson with Headmaster' day . . . Once a week he insists on coming into each class and boring us brainless, teaching us something **USELESS!**

Today we're doing science . . .

Science could be great if it was the kind of stuff you see on the telly. You know, like blowing things up or making potions that will shrink your teacher to the size of a pea.

BUT NO . . .

We're doing the boring, schooly–kind of science, which is **BAD** enough, but **EVEN WORSE** I have the painiest science partner of all . . . **AND NO, I'M NOT TALKING ABOUT WALTER!**

I have two words for you:

ANGEL FACE!!!

UGH! She's so tricksy!! She's as naughty as any **MENACE** and an even bigger MINX than Minnie . . . BUT . . . she's **Headmaster's daughter!** She's completely invincible when it comes to getting into trouble and **THAT** makes her dangerous!! It's like having **SUPER POWERS!!** She's so lucky!!

One time, in art, she spat a huge blob of blue paint at the back of Headmaster's head through a straw from the craft cupboard.

When the old twonk turned round and
glared in the direction it had come from,
the only two people on that side of the
room were Angel Face and Walter.
Even though Headmaster knew that
Walter would rather shrivel up and die
before doing anything naughty, he still
refused to believe it was his **DARLING,
ANGEL-FACED DAUGHTER.**

It was the one and only time that
Walter-Wet-Knickers got detention.
He cried for weeks . . . It was

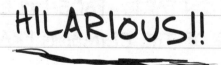

HILARIOUS!!

10.47 a.m.: HA! I've got the best plan. I'm going to menace Angel Face and there's nothing she can do about it. Normally she'd always do something to try and get me in trouble and stop me from making it to the climbing frame first at morning break. I'm ALWAYS first and today will be no exception. When the moment is right, I'm going to stick a mini stink bomb right into her test tube and everyone will think she's done a massive

BLOW-OFF!! Ha!

10.51 a.m.: There's only nine minutes to morning break!!!!! Nearly time to deploy

OPERATION FARTY-FACE!! I'LL BE KING OF THE CLIMBING FRAME FOR SURE . . .

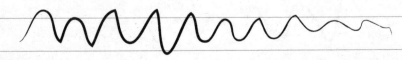

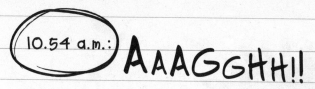 **AAAGGHH!!**

I DON'T BELIEVE IT! Just when I was about to stink-bomb Angel Face, she winked at me and then shoved all the science equipment off the front of the desk and smashed it on the floor. Then she threw herself across the table, knocking off everyone else's science stuff. It was **CLASSROOM CARNAGE.** There were broken bits of test tubes and Bunsen burner all over the place . . . **AND OF COURSE WALTER STARTED CRYING!**

Headmaster spun round and before I could say anything Angel Face went . . .

I HATE BEING OUT-MENACED!! ESPECIALLY
BY ANGEL FACE!!! Now I'm stuck indoors for
the whole of morning break and I can see her
at the top of the climbing frame. She even beat
Minnie the Minx to the monkey bars today, and
now she'll be KING OF THE CLIMBING FRAME
for the rest of the afternoon.

Walter's definitely not the only person I need
to keep an eye on this term. I'll get them both
before long, you watch . . .

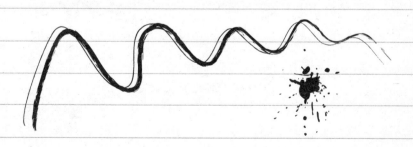

3 p.m.: Home time! The one good thing about being stuck inside at morning break was I had time to make a few posters.

Menacing Lesson no. 1036:

Use your detention time to plan your menacing.

I stuck one of these in Walter's school bag before leaving. He'll find it when he gets home . . . **HA!**

HAVE YOU SEEN THIS MONSTER?

Stories are spreading about sightings of a huge beast on Mount Beano that goes by the name of **BIG TOE**.

It is thought this sabre–toothed killer is gobbling up wafty little campers in their sleep. It especially likes the taste of WIMPS with a side serving of BOW TIES, GLASSES and BLUE JUMPERS.

CAMPERS BEWARE!

Friday

It's working! Today on my walk to.

Bash Street School me and Gnasher heard

Walter and his gang . . .

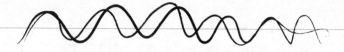

They're starting to get the heebie-jeebies.
This is perfect!!

By the time tomorrow arrives, they'll be
trembling in their Beanotown Butterflies
uniforms for sure!

Next stop, Dad's toolshed . . . I've got some
preparations to get on with before

THE BIG SCARE!!

THINGS I'LL NEED

- 2 broomsticks
- Nails and wood
- Dad's brightest torch
- Mum's old wellies
- My Mighty-Mouth-Megaphone
- Super-strength glue
- Bea's teddy bear

Phew! Got everything . . . You have no idea how tricky some of it was!

DROOL

POP!

Have you ever tried smuggling your little sister's teddy bear out of her bedroom? I tell you . . . it's no easy feat. Her room is loaded with booby traps . . .

She's turned into quite the **MASTER OF MENACING**. I'm so proud of her. Still . . . she's had **THE BEST teacher!**

Right . . . let's get building!

BIG-TOE FOOTPRINT MAKERS

Broom handle

Wellies

BIG Toe-shaped feet

Lots of sticky glue

9.30 a.m.: WE HAVE LIFT—OFF!!

I've just waved goodbye to Mum, Dad and
Gran . . . HA! Mum and Dad didn't look very
happy on the back of Gran's Charley Davidson
motorcycle . . .

From the tree house, I can see the Softies are in
Walter's front garden getting ready to go. This is
going to be the BEST day . . . I can feel it.

11 a.m.: We're making good progress and are already at the foot of Mount Beano. Following the Softies is **SO** easy. They keep stopping every five minutes to have tea and sandwiches.

Ha! BUM-FACES!!

11.26 a.m.: Ugh! We've stopped again . . . This time they're having lemon squash and cupcakes. They're like old ladies, those three.

11.28 a.m.: Me and Gnasher are going to slip past Walter and his pet wet lettuces and get ahead of them. I know exactly where they're heading. There's a clearing in the forest, near the river where me and my little sister Bea had water fights last time Mum and Dad took us on a day trip.

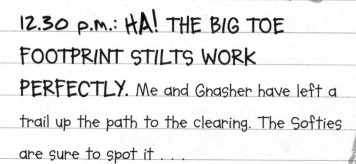

12.30 p.m.: HA! THE BIG TOE FOOTPRINT STILTS WORK PERFECTLY. Me and Gnasher have left a trail up the path to the clearing. The Softies are sure to spot it . . .

1 p.m.: Where are they? Another

GRANNY-BREAK, I suppose?

1.30 p.m.: This is **TOO** good to be true!!

I can hear them coming . . .

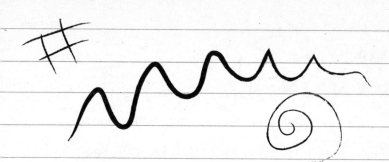

That's done it! They'll be pooing

their pants by the time the sun sets.

I'm going to take Gnasher and find

somewhere to hide and watch.

AGH! It's like waiting for

Christmas all over again!!

It's finally dark and the Softies have zipped themselves into their tent. Ha! They've been in there all afternoon and evening.

OK . . . Now to put the final part of the plan into action.

Let me introduce you to Bea's teddy bear. He's had a little makeover . . .

Monstrous hairdo

New nail claws

Here we go! With Gnasher's howling and a
little help from my dad's super-bright torch,
we'll have one **TERRIFYING** monster in no
time ... **HA!**

HA HA HA!!

That was the funniest thing I have **EVER**
seen! Walter and his cronies just went tearing
off back down the mountainside in their
onesies!! **TEDDY BEAR ONESIES!!**

SIGH! Sometimes life is just **SO** good . . .

Hmmm . . . I've just realized I'm starving!
Oh well. Since the tent is here and it's full of
the Softies' sandwiches, I think Gnasher and me
are going to have ourselves a little camping trip
for the night. I'll head home in the morning . . .

N'NIGHT!!!

11 a.m.: **Ugh!** I just got back from Mount Beano to find Mum in the front garden planting the first of this year's seeds . . .

I'd almost forgotten!

FLOWERS!

I need to get thinking about that one, my Trainee Menaces . . .

Oh . . . I dumped Walter's tent back over his garden fence with Bea's teddy inside. When he finds it, he's going to be so **CROSS!!** **Ha!**

Dear Mr Menace,

Thank you for placing your order with the **Mighty Mums** catalogue (gardening department). I'm afraid we are unable to send you your order of 10 BILLION SQUILLION packets of flower-killer as we simply don't have that much in stock. You must have the most terrible weed problem. Also where you were supposed to put your credit card number, you wrote BUM-FACE.

I wish you luck in the future and success with all your gardening endeavours.

Hilary Snuffle-Bush

Hilary Snuffle-Bush

OH BUMMMM!!

Tuesday

Taking Gnasher to the pooch parlour with Mum
to get him a spring trim . . . **BORING!!**

Not the next Wednesday . . . the Wednesday after that

Things just got a whole lot mushier . . .
BLEUCH!!

In a few days' time it's Valentine's Day . . .
I KNOW! THE SOPPIEST, SQUIDGIEST, MOST SOFTY DAY OF THEM ALL!

You won't find me sending any Valentine's Day cards to anyone . . . Well, not ones addressed from me anyway . . .

HA!

I think I might know just the way to get back at Angel Face after she got me into trouble **AGAIN!**

Dear Walter,

I can't keep it in any longer. My love is like a **BELCH** that needs to come out . . . **A REALLY BIG STINKY ONE!!**

You are the man of my dreams. You are the strawberry sauce on my ice cream. ~~You are a COMPLETE BUM-FACE!~~

You are the biggest, strongest, most gorgeousest <u>HUNK</u> I have ever seen at Bash Street School . . .

I love you a billion.

Smooches,

Your <u>TOP-SECRET</u> Valentine xxx

PS It's me, ANGEL FACE xxx

HA! That ought to do it . . .
I'll slip it into Walter's desk at school
this morning . . .

11.30 a.m.: UGH! Why is Walter such a
wuss? I saw him read the note and get all
blushy in class, but he still didn't go up to
Angel Face at morning break. She'll be so
embarrassed!! Ha! Serves her right!!

I think he's going to need a little bit more
encouragement . . .

WALTER,

MY SHMOOPSY-POO, MY HONEY-
BEAR, MY CUDDLE-PUDDLE . . .
WHY WON'T YOU TALK TO ME?
COME AND TELL ME HOW MUCH
YOU LOVE MY LETTERS AND DO
IT IN FRONT OF EVERYONE . . .
PLEASE!!

Valentine's Day

Hmmmm . . . Still nothing! I'll give him one last

little nudge . . .

My husband-to-be, ♡ ♡

It breaks my heart that you haven't stood

up in class and showed everyone the

letters I've sent you. I'd so love it if

you did . . .

I want everyone to know just how

much I love your guts!!

You could shout it out, or show them

to Headmaster, or photocopy them and

stick them all over school . . . I'd love that

SOOOOOOOOOOOOOOOOOOOOOOOO

much. That would be so romantic!!!

♡ ♡

Forever yours, ♡ ♡

Angel Face xxxx

AGH!!

I CAN BARELY BREATHE
FOR LAUGHING SO HARD . . .
WALTER DID IT!!
THE WAFTY-WORZEL DID IT!!

He stood up in the middle of Headmaster
De Testa's weekly lesson (this time it was
on dried-up riverbeds . . . **BORING!**)
and spouted everything in front of the
ENTIRE class . . .

And that, my MENACING MATES, is how you get your own back on tricksy headmasters' daughters!

(Sunday)

Ugh! Mum's outside planting even more FLOWERS!!

AND . . . from the tree house I can see loads of other mums and dads planting flowers in their gardens too!

I can almost hear the **TROMP, TROMP, TROMP** of an army of INTERNATIONAL Softies marching this way . . . and there are bugs too, which is a very bad sign!!

LOOK!

WAFTY WIFFLE BUG

STRIPY ZINGER STINGER

BOGEYBALL

SPRINGY GREEN THING

Menacing Lesson no. (751:)
Where butterflies go, SOFTIES are sure to follow!

The next Tuesday after the next Monday

11 a.m.: I'm so **MISERABLE!** It's morning playtime and I can't even bring myself to run out to the climbing frame or go play a game of footy with Curly and Pie Face.

Everywhere I turn there are flowers growing and butterflies fluttering. Beanotown is starting to turn into a dreamland for Softies . . . **IT'S JUST THE WORST!!!**

I tried firing spitballs at Walter with my pea-shooter, but it didn't cheer me up . . .

I tried putting superglue on the end of Creecher's red marking pen. When she realized she couldn't put it down, she flapped round the classroom like a demented turkey and splattered everyone with red ink, but it still didn't cheer me up . . .

WHAT'S WRONG WITH ME?

Yesterday we had the **BIG**, **STUPID** Easter 'Bring a can of something to school and put it on the table' day. I don't get all this Eastery stuff . . . It's something about tin cans and daffodils and a giant bunny?!?! **WHY CAN'T WE FORGET ALL THAT RUBBISH AND JUST EAT CHOCOLATE??** Sometimes I think I'm the only one who isn't crazy around here . . .

Every year we bring a can of something like beans, or tomatoes, or peaches, or pineapple chunks into school. Then we take the labels off so no one knows what's inside and then we swap them so we all get a surprise when we get home . . . SOME SURPRISE!

I think it's supposed to teach us something about sharing, but I haven't got a clue what!!!

Anyway . . . every year Walter brings in a can of his dad's El Shobbo Caviar, and **EVERY YEAR** Headmaster makes sure he swaps his can with Walter's.

So . . . this year . . . I switched Walter's can with a tin of Gnasher's **GRISTLY-GIBLET-JUMBLE** dog food when he wasn't looking and, sure enough, Headmaster just happened to swap with him.

I can just see Headmaster getting home tonight
and settling down in front of the fire with some
crackers and a can of GRISTLY—GIBLET—
JUMBLE . . .

But it still didn't cheer me up . . .

I'm **worried!** I don't find it

funny when funny things happen any

more . . . I don't feel like firing mud

balls at people's backsides with my

catapult . . . I don't enjoy shooting

spitballs with my pea-shooter . . .

I...

I...

I'M LOSING

MY INNER

MENACE!!

THIS IS AN
EMERGENCY!!

There's only one thing that can get me out
of this GRUMP and bring back my MENACING
MOJO in time to fight off all those SOFTY
hordes heading our way . . . AND IT'S THIS!!

BEANOTOWN
EASTER EGG HUNT

Head down to Beanotown Park this
Sunday for a morning of family
fun. Our special team of Easter egg
hiders is spending all of Saturday
night hiding hundreds of delicious
chocolate eggs for you to come and
seek out on Sunday morning.

WHAT FUN!!

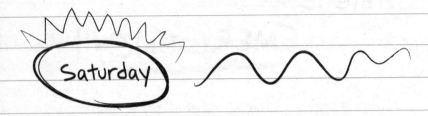

Saturday

6 p.m.: COME ON, DENNIS! YOU CAN DO THIS!!! It's the only way to bring back my inner menace . . . I've got an idea.

First things first . . . I've got some preparations to do if my plan is going to work . . . Mum and Dad are sitting watching their favourite programme on the telly . . . *ANTIQUES HOUR . . .*

Ugh!

BORING!

On the road out of town towards Bunkerton,
just before you get to Bunkerton Castle, is
a little chicken farm. I'm going to need a lot
of eggs . . .

Right . . . if I pedal on my bike as fast as I
can, I'll be back in time to catch the Easter egg
hiders in Beanotown Park.

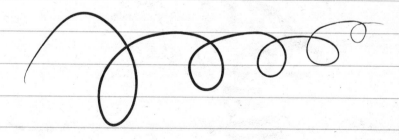

7.30 p.m.: Done! Now all I have to do is sneak into Dad's shed and dip all of these eggs in the big can of gold paint left over from last Christmas and they'll look just like the chocolate eggs they hide every year in the park.

9 p.m.: Check-check . . . This is Secret Agent Dennis, ready for action. Me and Gnasher are in our TOP-SECRET hiding place behind the rose bushes in Beanotown Park and the Easter egg hiders are already hard at work . . .

Now comes the fun part . . . Nothing can sniff out a chocolate egg like the super nose of an Abyssinian wire-haired tripe hound . . .

GO, GNASHER! GO!

SOMETHING STRANGE IS HAPPENING . . .
I CAN FEEL IT IN MY TOES AND IT'S
TINGLING UP MY LEGS . . . IS THAT MY
MENACING MOJO COMING BACK??

WE'LL SEE TOMORROW . . .

11 a.m.: Here we go . . . Most of the town has showed up for the **EASTER EGG HUNT . . . AND . . .** Walter and his cronies are right at the front of the egg-hunting party. This is going to be brilliant!

I FOUND ANOTHER!

11.01 a.m.: THEY'RE OFF!! Me and Gnasher are in the big oak tree right in the middle of the park. I can see everything from here! LOOK AT 'EM GO . . . ALL THOSE GREEDY LITTLE CHUBBERS!

Lunchtime: Aaaagh! I can't wait any longer!
All the eggs have been found . . . I can see the
Softies over by the swings . . . They've got to
crack on and eat them soon . . . WAIT FOR IT!
WAIT FOR IT!!

12.07 p.m.

HA!

THAT WAS

AMAZING!!!

IT'S BACK! MY TRAINEE MENACES, YOUR LEADER HAS RETURNED! I'M FEELING MORE MENACING THAN EVER!!

I nearly fell out of the tree I laughed so much . . .

DENNIS

THE PRANKMASTER GENERAL,

THE KING OF MENACING,

THE INTERNATIONAL MENACE OF MYSTERY,

HAS STRUCK AGAIN!!!

For a moment I thought they'd never eat their eggs . . .

But finally . . .

Ha! It's good to be a **MENACE** . . . You should've seen all the chaos . . . They went charging out of the Beanotown Park gates all covered in egg . . . I even heard Walter shout, **'RUN FOR YOUR LIVES, CHAPS! EXPLODING EGGS!'**

PAH!!

I'm feeling more inspired than **EVER** . . .
I'll take on all those hordes of **FLOWERY**
FLIM-FLAMS if it's the last thing I do . . .

I've got two weeks before the big unveiling of
the flowery town centre. Hmmm! There's work
to do . . . But before we start that I've got
a tree house full of **REAL CHOCOLATE**
EASTER EGGS to eat . . . **YUM!!**

Menaces x Softies - Flowers = ????

TWO
WEEKS
AND
COUNTING!!

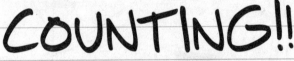

$$E = Softies^2$$

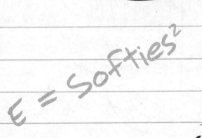

LET OPERATION BEANOTOWN BATTLE BEGIN!

TO DO LIST

- EAT CHOCOLATE

- WRITE IN MY MENACING DIARY

- STOP GROWN-UPS FROM GARDENING

- DEFEAT ALL THE SOFTIES

- KILL ALL THE FLOWERS

- STOP THE SOFTY HORDES FROM COMING

Hmmm . . . Things are looking tough . . . WITH
EACH PASSING DAY, ALL THE MUMS AND DADS
ARE PLANTING UP A STORM AND BEANOTOWN
IS STARTING TO LOOK MORE AND MORE . . .

BLOOMIN' AWFUL!!!
Ugh!

Walter's whole family has taken charge of the
town square. That's where the big unveiling is
going to take place and the exact spot that
all the international Softies will head for. I've
never seen so many flowers. They've planted
SOOOOOO many!

I've got to stop them . . .

Think, Dennis! THINK!

GLADIOLI GLADIATOR

SEED-ZAPPING EYE LASERS

PLANT-KILLER SPRAY GUN

ARRGH!

GARDEN SHEAR-HANDS

FLOWER-BED-STOMPING FEET

NOPE! TOO HARD TO BUILD!

Tuesday

AAGGHH! It's getting worse and worse . . .
today at school Mrs Creecher had us plant
seeds in anything we could get our hands
on . . . jam jars, yoghurt pots, old buckets . . .

You name it, we planted in it. Well, **THEY** did.
I just planted pebbles and bits of Gnasher's
hairballs in mine . . . I'm **NOT** helping those
SOFTIES!

It's still made no difference, though. They're
going to put all the planted pots on all the
window-sills in Beanotown Square. The Softies
are going to **LOVE IT!**

WHAT AM I GOING TO DO?!?!?!

ONE WEEK

AND COUNTING UNTIL

SOFTY -GEDDON!!

Only two days left until the grand unveiling of **BEANOTOWN** as the **BLOOMING BRILLIANT BOROUGH!!** I can see I'm not going to be able to do this one on my own.

BUT . . .

although I may not be able to stop the **SOFTIES** from coming here . . . with a little help from my friends, I can certainly send 'em packing!

Time to sort the **Menaces** from the **MUMSIES!!!**

I'm going to give out a few notes in class tomorrow . . . **CATAPULTS CROSSED!**

CALLING ALL MENACES

Our town is about to be taken over by the worst

kind of plague in the WORLD . . . SOFTIES!

IT COULD LOOK
LIKE THIS!!

SKIP! SKIP!

If you're cool, funny, **AMAZING**, adventurous,

brave, smart, strong or just generally **BRILLIANT**,

you'll know just how terrible that would be.

THIS IS THE <u>BATTLE</u> FOR BEANOTOWN!!

COME TO THE MENACE MEETING
TOMORROW NIGHT AT
DENNIS'S TREE HOUSE!

LET'S FIGHT FOR OUR FLOWERLESS FREEDOM!!

DENNIS

PS If you don't come, you're a complete **BUM-FACE!**

9 p.m.: **IT WAS BRILLIANT!** All the Menaces from Bash Street to Bunkerton showed up . . . Even Gran and Bea came and it was WAY past their bedtime. **I'M SO PROUD OF MY MENACING FAMILY!!**

BEA

BUT! EVEN **BIGGER** THAN THAT!!
ANGEL FACE CAME!!! She said . . .

We made plans . . . We swore oaths . . .
We prepared for battle . . .

PLUG

MINNIE
THE MINX

SPOTTY

SMIFFY

FATTY

TOOTS

SIDNEY

WILFRID 'ERBERT

GNASHER

ANGEL FACE

BRACE YOURSELVES,

MY MENACE SQUAD!

THE NEXT FEW PAGES
ARE GOING TO BE

A SOFTY
NIGHTMARE!!

Saturday: THE DAY OF RECKONING

My **MENACING TRAINEES,** the day has come. I woke up this morning to the sound of hundreds of posh Rolly-Roycey cars parking and **SOFTIES** of all shapes and sizes and ages heading through the streets to the town square. There are hundreds of them! HUNDREDS! IT'S THE MOST HORRIFYING SIGHT!

Thank goodness for my Wicked-Walkie-Talkie . . . All good Menaces have one and now we can chat and stay in touch as the town slowly fills up with **WET-LETTUCE WHINGERS.**

We have to get moving. Gnasher and me have to get to the alleyway behind Beanotown Square before we're spotted. It won't be long now . . . at 12 noon the Mayor is going to unveil the new Wafty Gardens in the middle of the square and all the Menaces are going to charge at once. Wish me luck, Trainee Menaces . . . I'll keep you posted . . .

11.45 a.m.: Check-check! This is Dennis the Menace coming to you live from just behind Beanotown Square. The Mayor is up on the podium starting his speech and all the Softies have gathered. It's like something from a really soppy horror movie!!

11.57 a.m.: The Mayor is <u>STILL</u> talking . . . GET ON WITH IT! MY BUM IS GOING NUMB!!!

11.59 a.m.: HERE GOES . . . THE MAYOR HAS THE CORD TO THE CURTAIN IN HIS HANDS!! HE'S GOING TO PULL IT . . .

12 noon:

CHARGE!!!

WE'RE OFF!! You should have seen the
Softies' faces as my **BRILLIANT**, flower-
squishing chariot tore across the garden . . .

The Softies started
screaming and
flapping like scared
chickens! They
darted off in all
directions . . .

Some tried to
scatter towards
Beanotown Park,
but Bea stopped
them . . .

POP! POP!

Other Softies tried to run through the garden,
but the Bash Street Kids got 'em . . .

Angel Face tied up Headmaster and bundled him
into a wheelbarrow . . .

Gran chased 'em up Bash Street . . .

AND . . . Minnie the Minx chased 'em

back down . . .

HA! THE SOFTIES RAN AWAY AS FAST AS THEY COULD!

There was only one last SOFTY to deal with . . .

WALTER!!!

Lucky for me, or UNLUCKY for Walter, Gnasher has the super-strongest nose in Beanotown and knew exactly where to find the BIG—WHINGEY—WIMPY—POSHO—PANTS!!!

Well, my **FELLOW MENACES** . . . **YEP!**
You're not Trainee Menaces any more. After
reading about the **BRILLIANT BEANOTOWN
BATTLE**, how could you not be fully qualified
Menaces?

WE DID IT! The Softies have all run
away . . . well . . . nearly all of them . . .

You should be very proud indeed . . .

Now don't forget what you've learned in the
BESTEST, MOST MENACING BOOK EVER!!
**I CAN'T WAIT TO SEE WHAT HAPPENS
NEXT TERM . . .**

**NOW GET OUT THERE IN YOUR OWN
TOWNS AND MENACE!!**

READY, STEADY, MENACE!!

I hope you got lots of menacing ideas from *Beanotown Battle*, fellow Menaces! There's plenty more inspiration in my first brilliant diary. Turn over for a reminder of the best Beanotown places for all you Masters of Menacing!

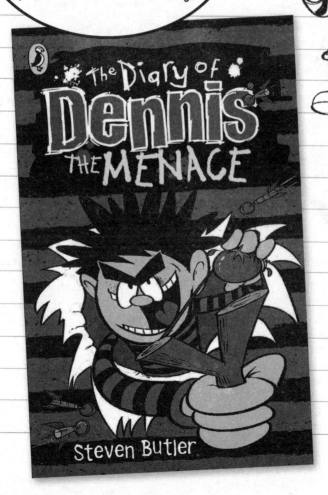

The Diary of Dennis the Menace

Steven Butler

THE TREE HOUSE

TOP-SECRET hideout for all Menaces everywhere

A GREAT VIEW of the Colonel's and Walter's houses

Perfect place to stash TOP-SECRET THINGS like chocolate and pocket money

Every good Menace has to have a base, and the best menacing bases are tree houses. It's amazing what funny things you can see from the top of a tree and, if Softies are sniffing about, you just have to pull up the ladder and they can't get anywhere near you, keeping you and your top-secret plans safe from snoopy, piggy eyes.

BEANOTOWN PARK

A squillion HIDING PLACES

Parks are a great stomping ground for Menaces. Beanotown Park is full of trees for climbing and hiding in, and has the boating pond and playground. The climbing frame in the playground is a fantastic lookout for keeping an

SWINGS (not very useful, but super fun)

BEWARE of the DUCK!

The BOATING POND for fishing, swimming and splashing SOFTIES

eye on Walter and his cronies and, if you need to top up your **MENACE-OMETER**, you can push them in the pond. Walter is terrified of pondweed and screams like a whingey baby every time . . . **Ha!**

BASH STREET SCHOOL

Now wait a minute!! I know what you're thinking
. . . School? **Has Dennis gone loopy?**

No! Dennis hasn't gone LOOPY! Think of all
the great menacing supplies that are there
for the taking. PAINT, INK, MODELLING
CLAY, PAPER, CHALK, DRAWING PINS!!
Never underestimate the importance of a quick,
secret trip to the school stock cupboard.

⸗ REMEMBER! ⸗

MENACES MEAN BUSINESS –

STOCK UP NOW!!!!

BEANOTOWN
The Quiz!

So you think you know Beanotown, do you? Well, now's your chance to prove it! Put your Beano brains to the test with this top quiz!

1. What is the name of the Bash Street School janitor's cat?
   - (a) Winston
   - (b) Egon
   - (c) Venkman

2. What number is printed on Calamity James's favourite jumper?
   - (a) 1
   - (b) 13
   - (c) 100

3. Which Bash Street Kid has the worst eyesight?
   - (a) 'Erbert
   - (b) Cuthbert
   - (c) Hubert

4. What kind of dog is Gnasher?
   - (a) Carpathian Stump-Nosed Haggis Pointer
   - (b) Ottomanian Long-Clawed Schnitzel Terrier
   - (c) Abyssinian Wire-Haired Tripe Hound

5. Who is Bananaman's secret identity?
   (a) Alan
   (b) Eric
   (c) Boris

6. What is the name of Little Plum's tribe?
   (a) Smellyfeet
   (b) Stinkybum
   (c) Pongybits

7. Who lives in Bunkerton Castle?
   (a) Sir Prince William
   (b) Lady Prawn-Sandwich III
   (c) Lord Snooty

8. Which Beanotown resident is famous
   for his black-and-red checked jumper?
   (a) Roger the Dodger
   (b) Tricky Dicky
   (c) Chequered Charlie

Answers: 1. a, 2. b, 3. a, 4. c, 5. b, 6. a, 7. c, 8. a

Gnasher's Canine Cackles

What do you get when you cross a dog with a telephone?

A golden receiver!

Why don't dogs make good dancers?

Because they have two left feet!

How did the little Scottish dog feel when he saw a monster?

Terrier-fied!

DON'T MISS MORE MENACING IN

The Diary of Dennis the Menace

Rollercoaster Riot!

Steven Butler

LISTEN TO AMAZING AUTHOR STEVEN BUTLER READ THE DIARY OF DENNIS THE MENACE!

DON'T MISS MORE MENACING IN